VINCENT VAN MOUSE

BY ANTHONY JOHN DESANTIS

Black CAT PUBLICATIONS INC.®

P.O. Box 7334
600 Franklin Avenue
Garden City, N.Y. 11530
www.blackcatpublications.com

Black CAT PUBLICATIONS INC.®

Dedicated to God .
Someone who never stops believing.

Text copyright © 2000 by Anthony John DeSantis
Artwork copyright © 2000 by Anthony John DeSantis
All rights reserved, including the right of reproduction
in whole or in part in any form.

ISBN 0-9712994-0-4

Black Cat Publication
P.O. Box 7334
600 Franklin Avenue
Garden City, New York 11530
www.blackcatpublications.com

Design layout by Carmine Namorato
All artwork by Anthony John DeSantis

Black CAT PUBLICATIONS INC.®

Dear Friends;

At Black Cat Publishing, publishing books is not our only purpose. We would like to take this opportunity to introduce ourselves and our intent.

The goal of Black Cat is to provide quality reading material to individuals of all ages but we would also like to make a difference to our friends, our pets.

Each year millions of animals suffer from unsuitable environments and, unfortunately, many do not survive. Lack of shelter, starvation, abandonment, and even abuse are the continuing problems these animals must face helplessly.

At Black Cat Publications we desperately want to make a difference to our pets in need and, with your help, we will. With every book purchased from Black Cat Publications we will donate a percentage to Animal Protection Foundations to help our friends in need.

Sincerely;

Carmine A. Namorato

VINCENT VAN MOUSE

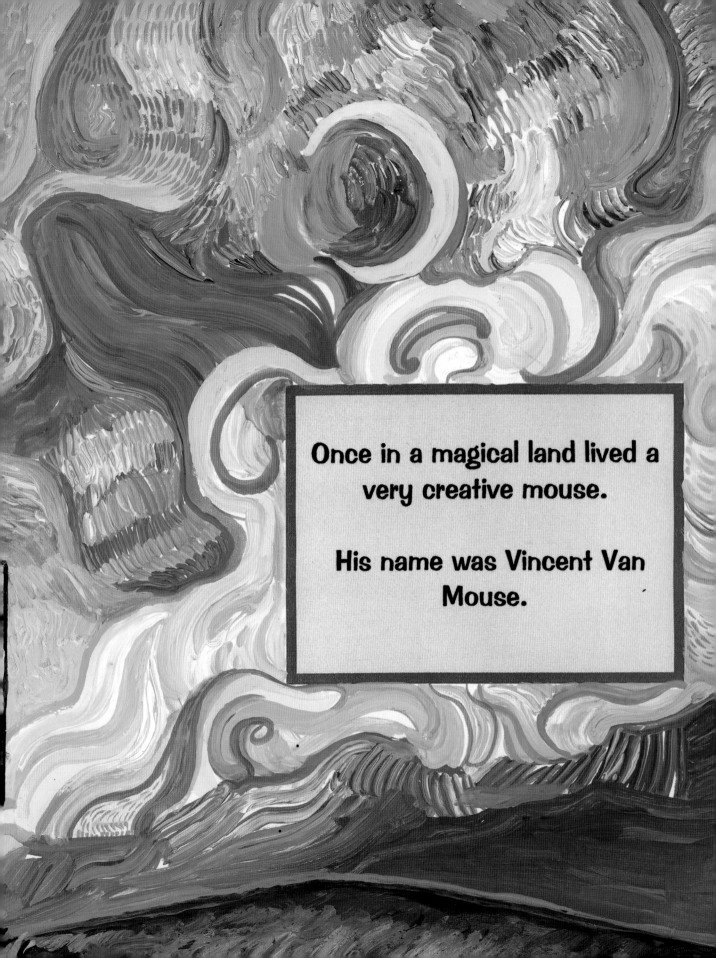

Once in a magical land lived a very creative mouse.

His name was Vincent Van Mouse.

Vincent Van Mouse was an exceptional artist.

One day the mice of Mousetown asked Vincent to paint a picture for Mouse Hall.

Vincent agreed.

Vincent knew he could paint a
beautiful picture.

He needed an idea.

Vincent thought what could he paint?

He decided to visit his friend Picasso Mouse, surely he would have some idea for Vincent.

Picasso Mouse painted objects like cubes and mice with strange faces.

Vincent admired his work, but it wasn't what he wanted to paint.

Vincent then paid a visit to his unusual friend Dali Mouse.

Dali Mouse painted dream-like pictures and melting clocks.

Vincent thought his work was different, but it wasn't what he wanted to paint.

Next Vincent paid a visit to his friend Monet Mouse.

Vincent thought how beautiful his work was, but it wasn't what he wanted to paint.

Monet Mouse painted lovely landscapes and pretty lily ponds.

THE WICKED MOUSE OF
THE WEST

Finally, Vincent paid a visit to his good friend Warhol Mouse.

Warhol Mouse painted colorful portraits and soup cans.

Vincent thought his work was great. What was Vincent going to paint?

"Oh, Warhol Mouse I must paint a wonderful painting for Mouse Hall. I'm not sure what to paint!" said Vincent.

"Why don't you paint a picture using your own style?"
replied Warhol Mouse.

Vincent walked and
walked.

He was tired of
thinking.

Just then Vincent realized what
a beautiful night it was.

Vincent looked up at
the sky.

All the stars were shining.

Suddenly, Vincent had
an idea.

It was a wonderful
idea.

Vincent went home and began to paint.

When he had completed his painting, Vincent realized that Warhol Mouse was right.

Vincent Van Mouse created a beautiful painting in his own style.

All the mice of Mousetown admired Vincent's painting.

There in Mouse Hall hung "Cheese Upon A Starry Night."

Vincent Van Mouse was truly a great artist.

ANTHONY J. DESANTIS
AUTHOR AND ILLUSTRATOR